For Kurt Dennis and Papa,

Your undeniable bond, right from the start, remains true—no matter the distance.

Love always,
Your Mama/Daughter

www.mascotbooks.com

Papa's Gift

©2021 Denise D'Angelo Roland. All Rights Reserved. No part of this publication may be reproduced, stored in a retrieval system or transmitted in any form by any means electronic, mechanical, or photocopying, recording or otherwise without the permission of the author.

For more information, please contact:
Mascot Books
620 Herndon Parkway, Suite 320
Herndon, VA 20170
info@mascotbooks.com

Library of Congress Control Number: 2020915450

CPSIA Code: PRT1120A
ISBN-13: 978-1-64543-592-1

Printed in the United States

Papa's farm is my favorite place.
My siblings all agree
it's a magical spot on a mountaintop,
unlike any farm you'll see.

It's a few hours in the car,
but we don't mind at all.
Because when we get to Papa's farm,
we're guaranteed to have a ball!

I'm not quite sure why it feels so calm—
it must be something in the air.
But the weather always feels just right,
and we arrive without a care.

I'm not even to the fun part yet—
you must see Papa's tractors and tools!
His equipment is handled carefully,
and we always respect the rules.

Papa has a farm dog, Charlie.
We love him as our own.
When he hears us pulling up,
he comes running with a bone.

After greetings, we head inside
to wash up and get some rest.
My room has the coziest bed.
Papa's farm is just the BEST!

Mornings at the farm begin
on the back porch all together.
There's a rooftop to protect our seats
in every kind of weather.

Blankets of snow or burning sun,
it's where we always start the day,
to share news, stories, and plan ahead
for the tasks that will come our way.

Mama has a favorite part:
holding mugs of something hot.
She loves when we can sit together
and be thankful for what we've got.

Soon after our quality time,
Papa's gang wants to get going.
We scurry along to get cleaned up
so we can harvest what's been growing.

Though we're rushed, it's not the same
as what I feel when I'm at home.
It's much more fun, and way less tense,
when no one's staring at a phone.

Charlie jumps up at attention.
He understands our cue.
His wagging tail gives us a giggle.
It says, "I'm coming, too!"

Papa tells us a secret code
to make the tractor start:
"Fire in the hole!" we say
as Dad follows in a cart.

We bumpity, bump down the mountainside
until we reach the gate.
We then hop out and scatter about
to pick something that tastes great!

Dad goes straight for the kale,
Addie and I grab the tomatoes,
Mama feels that squash is best,
and Sammy digs for potatoes.

Every person pitches in,
filling bins of our favorite crop.
We use the hose to give a rinse
before driving back up top.

Mama and Dad head to the kitchen
where they start preparing dinner.
The kids play games in Papa's den.
There's always a treat for the winner!

Suddenly, my mood feels low;
I don't feel much like playing.
Papa motions me to his chair—
he can read what my face is saying.

Wiggling up beside his lap,
I say, "I think I'm sad to go.
Tomorrow we'll be driving back.
Why can't home time feel this slow?"

Papa responds with a comforting hug
and a reassuring lift.
"Kurt, my boy, let me share with you
a very special gift.

"There's nothing here at the farm
that you can't take back with you.
All of these vegetables can grow at home,
and your father has tools, too.

It's clear to me what you love most
is when we spend our time connecting.
I know that you're the perfect guy
for some family redirecting.

"At dinner tonight, you could plan to share
your love for our time together.
Tell everyone your greatest hope
is to carve out time like this forever."

Staring back, my eyes grow wide.
I'm nervous to take the lead.
Then, Papa says with a loving hug,
"I'll be here for whatever you need."

Dinner time is finally called,
and we sit around the table.
I find the courage to share my thoughts
as best as I am able.

Mom and Dad nod with pride.
My siblings clap with glee.
I'm so relieved by their support
and to hear how they agree.

Bedtime brings me joy and peace,
as if there's been a shift.
I now understand what's special here:
it's the magic of Papa's gift.

Suggested Family Discussion

Recalling the message that you heard in
Papa's Gift, discuss the following questions with
your family members.

- In the first half of the story, why did you think that Papa's farm was Kurt's favorite place? What made you feel that way?

- When you were reading about Papa's farm, how did the description of the farm make you feel? What kinds of activities did Kurt and his family do there together?

- Do you have a favorite place to go with your family? What makes it your favorite?

- In the second half of the story, why was Kurt feeling sad? What was it about Papa's farm that was different from being at home?

- After speaking with Papa in his chair, Kurt was feeling nervous. Why was he feeling this way? What helped him to feel better?

- At the end of the story, what do you think "Papa's gift" really is? What activities can Kurt's family do at home together so that the magic of Papa's gift stays with them no matter where they are?

- When do you feel the most connected to your family? How does it make you feel to have time together without your devices?

Suggested Family Activity

Everyday life, particularly in this digital era, can sometimes feel overwhelming and fast-paced. The portability of our personal devices can make it a real challenge to unplug and reconnect with our loved ones. As a result, carving out meaningful quality time together has never been more important . . .

Visit our website at www.intentionallyunplugged.com to download a copy of our Intentionally Unplugged Family Workbook. Our guide will help you to facilitate a meaningful conversation with your family about establishing healthy tech boundaries in your home and in your lives. Take the first step bringing the magic of *Papa's Gift* back to your everyday life.

Make your own family contract! Together with your family, discuss ways to create healthy boundaries for technology use in your home.

Share your ideas on Instagram @intentionallyunplugged, and help other families, too.

Connect To What Counts.

Award-winning children's book author of *Please, Look up at Me* and founder of Intentionally Unplugged, Denise Roland is a veteran teacher and advocate for digital health. Denise attended Long Island University and graduated *summa cum laude* with a BA in psychology. She continued her education at Hofstra University, earning a MS in school counseling and a MS in health education, both with highest distinction. Today, she continues her twenty-year career in teaching on the eastern end of Long Island,where she lives with her husband and three kids, whom she loves to connect with more than anything.